ROC and ROE'S
Twelve Days of Christmas

by Nick Cannon

Illustrated by AG Ford

SCHOLASTIC PRESS · NEW YORK

On the first day of christmas,

Roc and Roe put on their Christmas tree
an angel with sparkly, shiny wings.

Our twins, Moroccan and Monroe (Roc & Roe), have brought so much joy into our lives. Mariah and I had so much fun putting this book together and we hope that you will have fun sharing it with your family.

Wishing you a happy and healthy holiday!

— Nick Cannon, Mariah Carey, and DemBabies

To my family: Mariah, Roc, and Roe. With Love, Daddy
— *Nick Cannon*

To the spirit of Christmas, bringing families
closer together every year.
— *AG Ford*

All rights reserved. Published by Scholastic Press, an imprint of
Scholastic Inc., *Publishers since 1920.* SCHOLASTIC, SCHOLASTIC PRESS, and
associated logos are trademarks and/or registered trademarks of Scholastic Inc.

No part of this publication may be reproduced, stored in a retrieval system, or
transmitted in any form or by any means, electronic, mechanical, photocopying,
recording, or otherwise, without written permission of the publisher. For
information regarding permission, write to Scholastic Inc.,
Attention: Permissions Department, 557 Broadway, New York, NY 10012.
Library of Congress Cataloging-in-Publication Data Available

ISBN 978-0-545-51950-2
10 9 8 7 6 5 4 3 2 1   14 15 16 17 18
Printed in the U.S.A.   44

First edition, November 2014
The text type was set in Shag Expert Lounge.
The display type was set in Circus Dog.
Book design by David Saylor and Charles Kreloff

On the second day of christmas,

Roe put on their Christmas tree

two singing Santas

and an angel with sparkly, shiny wings.

on the third day of christmas,

Roc and Roe put on their Christmas tree

three "pip" photos,

two singing Santas,

and an angel with sparkly, shiny wings.

On the fourth day of christmas,

Roc put on their Christmas tree

four skiing snowmen,

three "pip" photos,

two singing Santas,

and an angel with sparkly, shiny wings.

On the fifth day of christmas,

Roc and Roe put on their Christmas tree

FIVE GOLDEN BELLS,

four skiing snowmen,

three "pip" photos,

two singing Santas,

and an angel with sparkly, shiny wings.

On the sixth day of christmas,

Roe put on their Christmas tree

six festive fairies,

FIVE GOLDEN BELLS,

four skiing snowmen,

three "pip" photos,

two singing Santas,

and an angel with

sparkly, shiny wings.

on the seventh day of christmas,

Roc and Roe put on their Christmas tree

seven balloons with bows,

six festive fairies,

FIVE GOLDEN BELLS,

four skiing snowmen,

three "pip" photos,

two singing Santas,

and an angel with sparkly, shiny wings.

On the eighth day of christmas,

Roe put on their Christmas tree

eight tiny reindeer,

seven balloons with bows,

six festive fairies,

FIVE GOLDEN BELLS,

four skiing snowmen,

three "pip" photos,

two singing Santas,

and an angel with sparkly, shiny wings.

on the ninth day of christmas,

Roc put on their Christmas tree

nine jumping Jacks,

eight tiny reindeer,

seven balloons with bows,

six festive fairies,

FIVE GOLDEN BELLS,

four skiing snowmen,

three "pip" photos,

two singing Santas,

and an angel with sparkly, shiny wings.

On the tenth day of christmas,

Roc and Roe put on their Christmas tree

ten candy canes,

nine jumping Jacks,

eight tiny reindeer,

seven balloons with bows,

six festive fairies,

FIVE GOLDEN BELLS,

four skiing snowmen,

three "pip" photos,

two singing Santas,

and an angel with sparkly, shiny wings.

On the eleventh day of christmas,

Roc and Roe put on their Christmas tree

eleven teddy bears,

ten candy canes,

nine jumping Jacks,

eight tiny reindeer,

seven balloons with bows,

six festive fairies,

FIVE GOLDEN BELLS,

four skiing snowmen,

three "pip" photos,

two singing Santas,

and an angel with sparkly, shiny wings.

On the twelfth day of christmas,

Roc and Roe put on their Christmas tree

twelve chugging choo-choos,

eleven teddy bears,

ten candy canes,

nine jumping Jacks,

eight tiny reindeer,

seven balloons with bows,

six festive fairies,

FIVE GOLDEN BELLS,

four skiing snowmen,

three "pip" photos,

two singing Santas,

and an angel with

sparkly, shiny wings.

merry christmas to all!